T0131459

CYBERATTACK

MUKA

authorHOUSE®

AuthorHouse™
1663 Liberty Drive
Bloomington, IN 47403
www.authorhouse.com
Phone: 1 (800) 839-8640

Published by AuthorHouse 07/12/2018

ISBN: 978-1-5462-5124-8 (sc)
ISBN: 978-1-5462-5122-4 (hc)
ISBN: 978-1-5462-5123-1 (e)

Library of Congress Control Number: 2018908156

Print information available on the last page.

Any people depicted in stock imagery provided by Getty Images are models,
and such images are being used for illustrative purposes only.
Certain stock imagery © Getty Images.

This book is printed on acid-free paper.

Scripture quotations marked NIV are taken from the Holy Bible, New International
Version®. NIV®. Copyright © 1973, 1978, 1984 by International Bible
Society. Used by permission of Zondervan. All rights reserved. [Biblica]

My name is Muka. The past few years of my life have been very eventful, leaving a trail of lasting negative impressions of me with most people I met. I had way too many moments that led to a lot of burned bridges, broken relationships, and huge disappointments from friends and relatives. I have even been caught on the wrong side of the law. In a nutshell, I haven't been living up to acceptable standards of good behavior.

These past few years, I have been living in a foreign country, far from home and from anyone who truly knows me. I am going to tell you of one event that shook my world so badly it has taken me more than six months to make sense of it all and turn it into a coherent tale.

I can't honestly say when, how, why, or where all this began. But on November 29, 2016, I woke up just as I did every morning, with my radio tuned into a certain

Christian radio station. Mornings have been so bad these past few years that it took the radio playing encouraging songs and sermons just to get me out of bed. But this was a particularly bad morning. A few days before, one of the most important women in my life had died. My grief grew into a huge hole of loss filled not only with her death but with those of all the other people I loved, including my parents and two younger siblings. Amid this cascade of sorrow, I also had to face the fact that I couldn't even attend her funeral because it was thousands of miles across the ocean. My bank account was at zero. I had debts with every loan shark in town, and to top it off, I had piles of mail from debt collectors all over the country.

For the twenty-seven years of my life, I had nothing to show except a bunch of excuses, bad decisions, and very bad drama. Every day of the past few years, I felt a growing disappointment with myself. But on this day, each thought of the bad decisions I made amplified my disappointment to a degree I never felt before. I told myself to pull it together. I comforted myself with the fact that my writing was gaining a healthy following on social media and the internet. I even created a Facebook page dedicated to community development. So I told myself there was hope I could turn things around. To reinforce this little hope, I turned to the one source that had offered me encouragement every morning for the past few years—the Christian radio station.

On air was a preacher I had listened to many times before. I suddenly realized he was talking about my Facebook page posts! It was very flattering. A moment ago I felt very insignificant, and here was a renowned pastor talking about my posts on a radio station thousands were tuned into.

This moment was short-lived. I was someone who once knew God, he continued, but turned away from the path. This preacher even broke down one of my posts line by line, talking about how my writing style was a scheme to attract followers and was sinful and rebellious to God. I found myself believing his words. My messed-up life was evidence of their truth. He went on talking until my mind became clouded and taken over by my earlier feelings of disappointment. I was convinced I was a big disappointment to my friends, to my relatives, to society, and now even to God.

I sat down, so overcome by guilt and shame that I felt the need to be exorcised or something. How did the preacher or the show's producers even know of my existence? Then I remembered the time I got in touch with one of the DJs at the station to show my appreciation for the work they were doing. They must have looked me up on Facebook and found that I was admin for a page with quite a decent following. But why wouldn't this pastor just approach me to talk about my posts? I wondered if I was too bad to even reach out to. He had to make a radio program to dent my work.

After a while, I pulled it together. I reasoned that he is a man and entitled to his opinion, and opinions are not facts. But it was still very discouraging that one of the people I looked to for inspiration was now attacking me. Once again, self-doubt was brewing in my mind. Instead of fortifying me with hope that morning, the radio program had ended up eroding the little I had. I was back to zero. My mind consumed with memories of bad decisions and negativity.

And that was how my morning started. I jumped out of bed and walked to the living room. I lived on the second floor of a two-story townhouse. It was time to check on my social media activity and how my page was doing. I sat on the couch to use the computer, which was connected to the plasma TV. I quickly logged into my account, and what I found did nothing to restore calm to my state of mind.

It appeared all my Facebook friends in a fifty-mile radius of my address woke up to write insulting posts about me on Facebook. My newsfeed from top to bottom was filled with offensive posts all targeted at me. It was like they all called one another and agreed to do this that morning. The shock made me question my senses. I thought my mind was playing tricks on me. It was unbelievably weird that one of the top preachers gave a sermon about me and that now all this stuff was in my newsfeed from people I needed support from.

I immediately emailed one of my pastor friends and told her something weird was going on. I told her I wasn't exactly sure what it was, but I thought I was seeing and hearing things that couldn't be real. She told me to stay put, and she would come see me as soon as possible.

The insults were too much and very personal. I felt my privacy had been violated on the most extreme levels. I didn't want to look anymore. Feelings of being a reject flooded my mind like water over a dam. This was a huge blow to my sense of trust.

Then rage started burning in me like a gaseous fire. I looked at Facebook, but this time I picked up something different—a very tiny discrepancy from its usual newsfeed, which I looked at many times every day on different devices. So I knew the setup very well. I could tell it was fake! My friends were not making these posts. They were coming from a single source in a stream that mimicked the usual Facebook newsfeed with real people. Despite my limited knowledge about computers and the internet, I quickly concluded that it would take a lot of computer-talented personnel and many resources to force-feed a stream between my Facebook address/ID and the real Facebook newsfeed with my real friends. Moreover, it would take a lot more computing power to hold the stream there to give me enough time to see it and ignite certain feelings. Whoever was doing this was no average person … or people.

This realization scared me beyond what I imagined to be the furthest point fear could go. My morning started with a popular radio preacher condemning me, and moments later, I underwent a cyberattack of hurtful insults. The people behind it worked so hard to make me think the posts were coming from my friends. I was dealing with people using their mighty power to attack me for reasons I couldn't yet figure out. My mind was filled with questions about who they might be.

Then I remembered some six or eight months ago while I was in another city. I thought I saw someone spying on me, watching and following me all over the city. It was like I was supposed to lead him somewhere, perhaps to an illegal underground group. I didn't bother much with the situation because I knew I wasn't hiding anything. I was acquainted with so many people from different parts of the world and with different behaviors, lifestyles, religions, races, and so on because I liked meeting people and listening to their stories. I figured it was my eccentric and friendly nature that led to government surveillance to make sure I wasn't a threat to society. I wondered if this wasn't just paranoia, but I failed to see it as coincidence when I saw the same person in different parts of a city with a population of more than six million. Given the logic that this memory was serving, the radio program, the computing power, and the amount of effort and time that went into putting the stream together, I concluded that only a government was that powerful and must have been behind what was happening to me that morning. I wasn't too quick to point out which government it was because I didn't have solid evidence to substantiate that claim. I also had knowledge that countries agree to open borders with each other to allow operatives to spy on individuals of interest without giving a reason to the host nation. So I wasn't sure if it was the government of the country I am from, the government of the country I was in, or maybe some government unknown to me. My other consideration was the possibility of governments working together being behind this.

The thought that I was an enemy to established political powers and that it was the reason why the pastor freely made that program and openly condemned me and my writing was supported by the possibility of my Facebook page being a threat to the order of economics and power in place. After all, I strongly spoke against inequality, and I advocated for freedom and unity. But I still felt it was within my rights to speak and share information, and this attempt was a violation to my freedom of speech. Moreover, given the amount of personal information in that stream, I felt that my privacy was breached and that this cyberattack was evident of that. Then my anger was at red alert. I felt my head boiling at the hypocrisy of many public figures, such as the pastor who made the radio program against me. I was so angry that my body started shaking, and that anger increased with a lack of physical reach toward these people so I can let it out on them until I was completely out of control and responded the only way that I felt I could. It must have been because this whole thing was started by a radio sermon against me. At about 2:00 p.m., I started posting Bible verses on Facebook at a rate faster than I could type. Post after post after post, I flooded my Facebook time line with more Bible verse posts, and then I switched to rants upon rants about Christians, Muslims, and people of all religions, mostly about how sinful and judgmental they were just like everyone else. My rants went on to how society could fail to follow these teachings and be judgmental in the same manner. I then started ranting of how small and venerable I was and how it was unfair that powerful people were treating me the way they were.

It wasn't until after people started commenting on my Facebook rant and messaging me that I realized how much my anger had taken me over and narrowed me into acting on impulse. My earlier conclusion was much like Ernest Rutherford when he shot a beam of alpha particles on a sheet of gold foil and hypothesized that the gold foil would repel all of the alpha particles. My conclusion before making the posts was that what I was typing would fall on their fake stream and that none of my friends would see my rants. The opposite happened, and now all the people on my friends list saw the posts I had made without stopping for a straight ten minutes and probably flooded their entire newsfeed. Oops! My day was now turning into a nightmare as reactions from my friends demanded an explanation. Some of them were pissed off, and some were mocking me. This became a perfect moment for anybody to unleash their negative or malicious words about me without worry of consequence. I realized how I made my problems worse now. I opened up a battlefront when I was being whooped on the other ones. I quickly walked inside my apartment, both hands holding my head. I quickly walked down the stairs and out the door and sat out on the concrete stairs of the whole building. I contemplated the impeding confrontations that were yet to come my way from friends and relatives. I then observed the street, feeling as if a crowd with pitchforks and stones would soon appear to purge their anger with me. But all I saw was the construction crew that was doing renovations to our building. They had been fitting new windows in my apartment building for the past fourteen days. I then looked at the owner of the company, observing him with extreme suspicion, wondering if all this renovation work was just a front to keep close surveillance on me. I then began to think that maybe during the time that I thought they were putting new windows in my apartment, they were actually installing micro cameras in my apartment to watch and study my behavior when I was alone. I even considered a possibility of being on a live broadcast and people watching me.

As all these thoughts went through my mind, I looked at the crew with extreme hate. There were people passing, and my hatred extended to them as well. I didn't want to be outside anymore, so I went back into my apartment. As soon as I got back in the apartment, I observed more and more comments and messages coming. I had not wept in years, but in that moment I cried tears of anger because of the cyberattackers. All this mess was their fault, and only God knows how much I wanted to retaliate. But how do you fight someone or something you can't see? I then figured it best to try to deescalate the social media uproar against me. I responded to a few texts from some very close friends and family asking them to disregard what I said with those posts. I explained to them that I was being cyberattacked by some unknown people. One of my friends asked if I was involved in politics because that was when people would launch an attack on that scale. I explained to him that I wasn't involved in political matters and that it was maybe because of the Facebook page. I then started making apologetic Facebook posts because most of my friends followed a religion that I had spoken ill of. But these posts were just making things worse because they attracted more outrage, mockery, and worry from most of the people. Then the cyberattackers responded with another stream in my newsfeed with posts of cartoons, videos, and images mocking and reminding me of my predicament. The underlying and precise message in this stream was that I was messed up and the whole world knew of it. The considerations I made about my apartment having micro cameras embedded into the walls took over my mind. So I sat quietly, thinking about all of it. I thought of all the mistakes I had made, especially the many times when I was arrested and convicted of some misdemeanors. I imagined this attack as the justice system's alternative to jail time, given that prison was overcrowded and the government didn't have the resources to support the facilities. So maybe this was the government's way of teaching me a lesson to set me right. Then I realized that it was just my belief in humanity fighting to stay alive because my conscience was clear of any wrongdoings that warranted this kind of torment. Besides, I had paid my fines with the justice system, so my debt is settled with the law.

The door to my apartment rang, and my adrenaline skyrocketed as thoughts of what I might face ran through my mind. A cousin of mine emerged from the staircase and walked into the living room. I then remembered that a few days ago he had asked me for a key to my apartment so he could come by even when I wasn't there. As I sat on the couch, I was already getting a feel for him. He was here to figure out why I was making such posts and possibly the best way to approach me with the matter. He stared at me and could tell that I wasn't quite my usual self that day. So to break the awkward silence between us, he started talking. I was surprised that his first words weren't a confrontation. I think he must have figured I wasn't in a state to deal with that. He talked about life and experiences and many other things without mentioning anything to do with Facebook or my state of mind. I could tell that he was holding back what he really felt like saying. I will admit my mind was largely battling the mysteries surrounding my situation. But whatever attention I was giving him, I got a feeling about the mess I was causing with the family. So I kept quiet and let him carry on talking. Then he called my name and wryly said something that made me give him my full attention. He told me he knew exactly what was going on and the situation I was in because he had been there and also gone through it.

"Really?" I said, and he said yes. Then he added that it had happened to a few other family members. To me, this meant the family knew about this and nobody thought of mentioning that it would happen to me. And if it had happened to a few other families, why perpetrate it? I was now convinced that my family had a hand in this cyberattack. I was now starting to connect my family's Christian heritage to what the pastor on the radio was saying about how I rebelled against God. I concluded that my family obviously gave that pastor the go-ahead to make that radio program and then worked with the established political powers of some unknown country or countries to launch this attack on me. Now in that moment I felt betrayed, and the rage I was feeling earlier multiplied. I felt really hurt. Even if my family thought so little of me, this was taking things too far. I felt I would never let someone I hate go through the kind of torment I was experiencing. I felt hate with all my heart and mind. For a second or two, I felt like pouncing on my cousin like an animal and tearing him apart. But I told myself to keep calm. I knew overreacting could give people who weren't involved something to say about me. So I crossed my arms really tightly to keep myself cool as he kept on talking. I kept quiet the entire time until he decided to leave.

After he left, feelings of betrayal and abandonment crept up through my skin like a winter chill. I started thinking about my travels and involvement with some people in my country and overseas and how it was all a setup that led exactly to this moment. The moments that I was applying for my visa, the people who helped me at the embassy, to when I travelled and started making friends at school and work and every day until that hour of that day. I was beginning to feel nostalgic of my simple background living in the village and in the slums. The doorbell rang, and my thoughts were cut short. With great hesitation and apprehension, I opened the door, and standing there was the pastor friend I had called earlier in the day. She was with a certain pastor that I was acquainted with, but I didn't know a lot about him. So he was more like a stranger. But I let them into the apartment. They sat down and both of them were looking at me with great concern. So my pastor friend spoke first, reminding me of the many times that she told me I had great potential and also mentioning how the devil was after me because of that fact. I said nothing back because I remembered her saying that many times and regarded those words as a mere natural response to a situation she wasn't aware of because I was dealing with people using computer algorithms, radio stations, and high intelligence with human behavior. I thought about how there was no demons, ghosts, or devils. It was just a bunch of men and women who had just decided to band together and launch a stealth attack on me. But what the other pastor said multiplied my paranoia, mistrust, and fear. The pastor asked me why he was seeing me going to hell, and for the first time, I responded by repeating his question and asking if he really saw me going to hell. And he said yes. I then started thinking about my vision. I looked around my apartment and didn't see myself going to hell. I was scared and confused because going to hell was something I didn't want, so him seeing me going to hell without me seeing that reality really impacted me. I felt the panic you feel when someone warns you of something dangerous like a venomous snake or poisonous spider or scorpion about to strike. This was what was going on in my mind, but with my adrenaline at my highest. I don't know long this mental panic lasted, but I started reasoning eventually. I had started my morning by listening to a pastor on radio who had regard for my well-being by offering his criticism and condemnation, and now there was another pastor telling me that he saw me going to hell. For all I knew, they could all be in on this together along with the cyberattackers. My trust in my pastor friend dropped to zero as well. Then the feelings of betrayal surfaced. I felt cornered with no one to trust and nowhere to go. I quickly concluded that the only reason the pastor in my apartment saw me going to hell was because he was planning to send me there himself, or maybe he knew someone who would. I looked at him as he looked back at me intently, expecting him to strike at any moment. I stayed on that couch because I didn't want to suddenly get jumpy and find that they weren't carrying any weapons or weren't even going to strike me. Plus even if he was a pro, I was close enough to reach him if he decided to pull out a gun. Then my pastor friend asked that we pray. As we prayed, I didn't close my eyes completely because I was watching both of them. After the prayer they stood up to leave, and I walked them out. I stopped at the door and locked it behind them.

When I came back into the living room and sat on the couch, I was convinced beyond a reasonable doubt that what the pastor said about me was a threat that I shouldn't take lightly. Adrenaline was rushing through my body at lightning speed as thoughts of dying clouded my mind. I contemplated the situation a little bit more in hopes of trying to figure out a way to avert my impending death. I was being spied on by supposedly government operatives. A preacher openly made a radio program declaring me a rebel against God, supposedly working with my family, and now my pastor friend has betrayed me, aligning with someone giving me a subliminal message about me going to hell. Was the whole world against me? I had no one to turn to for help. So I did what I thought was the only thing I could do. I logged back into my Facebook, and in a desperate attempt to reason with the people behind this attack, I started making Facebook posts stating that I had tried my best to be an upstanding citizen. I even talked about how I failed to take responsibility for my actions. Basically, all the posts were stressing an idea that I wasn't their enemy. Then another stream filled my newsfeed all posts talking about death more like that was the social media day trend, like how when a big celebrity dies or tragedy then everyone starts RIP posts and floods everyone's newsfeed. But in my case, they were showing the death of an abstract fictional character who was an outstanding member of the community and who spoke against violence and called for a ceasefire in times when people might pick up guns and fight. In the midst of all this panic and fear, I interpreted what the pastor had said about seeing me going to hell as their message of what was going to happen to me. And then it occurred to me that my pastor friend's field of study was neural science, and my suspicions deepened. With this experience starting with the sermon on the radio and the streams, I started thinking of the applications of neurology, psychology, and sociology and how it all fit with my current situation. But these thoughts were interrupted when I discovered that the computer webcam on top of the TV had been on the whole time throughout the day. I got up and then looked into it. I figured that the reason the attackers were so effective with getting under my skin was because they were watching me the whole time. So I looked into the webcam and did what I guess any reasonable man would do. I apologized, talking about how I was sorry and how I had learned a big lesson from this experience. I then said to them that if all this was about the Facebook page, I would delete it and do whatever they asked of me if they promised to spare my life. I then said that if I was beyond mercy and they chose to kill me anyway, I was okay with that. I understood if they needed to make me an example of what happened to people mess with them. I then asked that they not involve any of my family, especially my siblings. I assured them that they had problems of their own that were already too big for them to handle. Then I sat down on the couch, my down, and I kept talking, asking them to show mercy. And then my TV screen lit up. There was a pop-up at the bottom center of my screen. I was logged into Facebook with the living room computer, but I could tell that this pop-up was not attached to Facebook. It was more like how you open a computer window but then open another, and for a time they overlap each other like layers. This was a very interesting discovery because I had originally thought that they could only get to me through Facebook pathways and reach me only when my Facebook was open. It was clear to me that they had sent that pop-up through my IP address. The message showed me the information and disappeared like it was never there. They were instructing me to copy and paste the words on the pop-up and post on Facebook. I read the words, and it turned out they wanted me to claim responsibility for a plane going down, and alongside those words were some Arabic words. My heart skipped a beat or two. I didn't know if this plane crash was real or not, if it had already happened, or if it was yet to happen, but I knew what posting that on my wall would do. I jumped up from my feet like a cat in flight mode and looked into the webcam and said no bluntly. Then the pop-up started flashing aggressively with an arrow prompting me to do as they said or else. At this time I began to question my earlier thought that it was the government or some governments working together behind all this. My fear and panic climbed to a higher level as I thought. Would established powers go so far as incriminating an innocent man just to show the public that they were doing their jobs by putting down threats to society and in doing so, maintain their firm grip on power and control. I assumed that I was chosen to be the fall guy for this operation at this time, and I started thinking of how my personality and activities made me perfect for this trap. So I got caught in between the great need to stay alive by any means necessary and the consequences of me posting what they were asking me. I then started playing out a few scenarios in my head if I posted what they asked. First, the public was very sensitive to terrorism, and posting that would automatically prove me guilty in everyone's eyes. Within minutes, every law enforcement across the country and possibly the whole world would be on high alert (APB) and given permission to use lethal to put me down if necessary. And even if I ended up getting lucky and being arrested, the excessive torture that would be applied would render me brain dead or kill me. Amnesty International would not even be close enough to have a say in proceedings. At the same time, I would make negative international headlines, and radio programs like the one that the pastor played would become a sensational topic. Psychology and sociology experts would dissect my background and gather huge amounts of information to prove the validity of these actions. This would probably trigger TV debates among intellectuals. It would all escalate toward my family and friends. They would be rounded up and put through rough interrogations and screenings that would damage and traumatize them for many years. The pop-up was still flashing, and I was still saying no, thinking about my attackers with a new perspective. After posting, I was sure they would quickly move in to pick me up and relocate me with a new identity while the public outcry and media frenzy played itself out. But posting what they wanted would be adding fuel to the fire against Arabs and Islam, especially since the pop-up had some Arabic words, and that was too high a price to pay just to save my own neck.

So after finalizing my thoughts, I looked into the webcam and said no loudly. I also said to them that if they wanted to kill me, then they should go ahead and do it. I assured them there was no way I was posting that. From that moment on, I was expecting death. Adrenaline rushed through my body like an electric current, and I was in fight-flight mode as I thought about how I would meet my death. At the same time, I wondered what my attackers' next move might be. I never thought my mind would have all these thoughts. I then arrived at a theory that their next move would be to try to force-feed my computer and send incriminating messages to my social media accounts while they contacted the authorities and reported me as a possible terrorist. I then started thinking that maybe the pretend construction crew that was doing renovations had already transferred files onto my computer with incriminating information such as flight plans, building schematics, and systems specs. What if law enforcement agents were already on their way with a warrant to bash through my door and search everything in my apartment. Those files on my computer would make me look guilty, and anything I said would not matter. And then the public outcry and media frenzy started playing in my mind again. Every atom and molecule in my body was screaming for me to get out of that apartment and run, so within seconds, I was out on the street. My eyes and ears and skin were at high alert. It was now around 6:30, so with every car that drove past me, I peered through the beaming lights and through the windshield, counting the number of people inside, memorizing what they were wearing and searching their body language for any indication of hostility. I was approaching all of the blind spots on the street with extreme caution, thinking that someone might pop out with a gun. My pace was faster, and I analyzed distant dark spaces, trying to locate any figures in case a sniper was hiding there. My senses narrowed, trying to pick up sounds that clicked or resembled clicking or rattling or the sounds of small explosions like gunshots or an RPG. Every moving branch in a tree or small animal footsteps rattled me. My sense of smell was in constant search for any slight increase in the amount of carbon monoxide in the air. On top of all that, I was also calculating my options where I could go. I was still too paranoid to trust the government, given my strong suspicions of them. I couldn't go to my family, given that my cousin had told me about his awareness of the plot. I had zero cash, so my primary means of running was on foot since I didn't have a car. I felt like a soldier behind enemy lines. My senses heightened to a point that I could see inside a drop of water from a hundred feet away, hear the footsteps of a bug, and taste the air like juicy steak. I was venerable and out in the open.

I then realized that I had been walking for ten minutes. I must have been going toward downtown out of impulse or as a survival instinct, but the thought of where I was at that time made me realize that I was five-minute walk away from my workplace. So I did what I thought was my best option. I went to my workplace, and when I arrived at the front entrance, I saw my two supervisors through the glass doors at the security desk. My adrenaline spiked as I tightened more and more into fight-flight mode. I became increasingly apprehensive as I stepped closer and closer to the glass door to make my presence known. At the exact moment my two supervisors saw me, I was studying their body languages for any sign of distress or changes to determine whether to flee or stay. My two bosses greeted me with friendliness and a sense of calm that surprised me. After all, I hadn't shown up for work at 5:00 p.m. or called to let them know I wasn't coming in, so I told myself that maybe they were just in a good mood. I went straight into talking about how they knew me well. I wanted them to believe in me and everything good they had seen in my behavior at work. I also emphasized how I worked well with other people regardless of differences and how I could never be of any harm to anyone. Then one of my bosses asked me to calm down and told me to meet them in the office. We walked to the elevators, and somehow my apprehension and paranoia of them subsided. I took their sense of calm as an indication that they were oblivious to my earlier offensive rants on Facebook. As soon as we got into the office, I asked that they call the police and that they stay with me until the police took me with them. I figured that was the safest way of getting into police custody, given that I already assumed the authorities were at my apartment and on high alert. My hopes were that if I could tell my side of the story early enough, at least one or two police officers at the precinct would believe me regardless of the evidences that the cyberattackers had planted at my apartment. I kept rushing my two bosses to call the police like an impatient kid crying for his toy, but they just stood there, looking at me like I was crazy. It then dawned on me that they must have gotten wind of my earlier Facebook posts. I didn't have a cell phone, so I asked if I could use their office phone. Then they told me the office phones had stopped working a long time ago. At this point, I realized that I was hitting a brick wall with them, and then one of my supervisors said something that got me thinking. He said everything that was happening was just the result of people playing with me. Questions about which people he meant swept through my mind like a whirlwind. I was starting to suspect their sense of calm. Both of them were now at the top of the list of suspects supporting or working with the cyberattackers. After all, one of the posts in the stream talked of a moment with the very two people who were in the office with me now. We were on a different floor the night before, and my two supervisors were making fun of me in what was quite an embarrassing moment. So either one or both of my supervisors got in touch with the cyberattackers and revealed the details of that joke so that they could put in one of their mock posts as a way of letting me know that they had people everywhere. Another theory was now starting to brew in my mind. Given the amount of computing power that the cyberattackers had, I deemed it possible for them to hack into the building's surveillance systems and watched me at work. They may have seen that joke moment with the supervisors. With these two theories in mind, I thought about the motives that my two supervisors would have in taking part in this elaborate attack on me. I didn't know a whole lot about them, and we had only worked together for just six months.

The single important detail that registered in my mind was that they had served in the government before. It was believable enough to me that their involvement could have been the result of someone ordering them to report a recent moment with me. I was also beginning to consider the fact that maybe all this was an operation meant to shake me up so that I would spill any information that the government thought I was hiding too well. I imagined that maybe they had pegged me as a possible spy or terrorist with connections all over the world. So I was connecting all of the dots leading to this moment with my two supervisors. Now what was I going to do about all this? My first thought was to ask one of the supervisor about who just playing with me, but I quickly concluded that the chances of him giving me that information were thin. Using force or aggression would just make my situation worse. They could possibly have me locked up for lunacy and being a danger to others then. I looked at my two supervisors, studying their facial expressions as they grinned like performers, restraining myself from doing anything rash or making accusations that might make my situation worse. I held back my impulses and went along with theory number two. Maybe the cyberattackers had hacked into the building's surveillance systems. So I gave my two supervisors the benefit of the doubt that they were just referring to the comments on Facebook from different people. That was when an idea hit me about Facebook. I could prove the nature and extents of those streams by observing my friend's Facebook walls as I used another Facebook account from a different IP address. Then I could see if there were any signs of them playing a part in all this. So I asked my supervisor if he had Facebook, and right away he said yes without even thinking about why I was asking. I then said to him that I needed to show him something, and he obliged my request as if it was coming from a king. He logged into his Facebook, and I asked him to search for one friend's name that the cyberattackers had used repeatedly in their first stream. As we scrolled down my friend's time line, there was nothing that resembled anything close to what I had seen that morning. I also checked this friend's Facebook wall because all the posts were always public so that anyone with a Facebook account could see the posts. That was my first significant factual findings about the cyberattackers trying to break my trust in friends. I then concluded that even my supervisors saying that these people were just playing with me was nothing more than a natural impulse, given that their knowledge of my situation only went as far. I kept on thinking up more scenarios and considerations as my supervisor scrolled farther and farther down my friend's time line until he finally asked what exactly we were looking for. I felt like telling him every little detail, but given that he probably thought I was having a mental breakdown, I didn't think he would believe me. Besides, I also didn't have the time. So I only told him to stop and said that it was really nothing. He then got up from his chair and said okay, obviously confused that I had asked him to do something that didn't make sense at all. I then told them I was ready to leave, and so I left.

As soon as I hit the sidewalk, there was a slight uplifting feeling. I was sure beyond reasonable doubt that it wasn't my friends making those posts. My hope and belief in humanity was elevated again. I was a little bit less scared as I walked the streets. But this respite was overtaken by the thought of the real dangers that I thought I was still in. I imagined that the cyberattackers still had a plan in play and that I would still be implicated in way that would change my friend's opinions about me. It would not be about what I say but rather about what things look like, and the short-term damage would be beyond recovery. My fear and panic came back, and I was in fight-flight mode, my hearting beating faster this time and my senses heightened more than before. It was my little belief in humanity that gave the courage to go to the police station. Besides, it was also the best option I thought I had. I was praying that regardless of how things turned out or if the cyberattackers had already contacted them, at least one or two will believe me. Then I started thinking that I could be walking into a trap. I thought of how there could already be an APB with my name and picture and orders to shoot at first sight. But all these thoughts didn't stop me from moving toward the police station. When I saw the building, however, I stopped about a hundred feet away. I then started looking for any signs of frenzy, but I saw nothing. As a matter of fact, the premises were as calm as a sleeping baby. Then I slowly started moving closer, attentive and cautious. Forty feet away at the edge of the concrete staircase to the entrance, I stopped dead as the building door opened. My hair froze, and I could feel the electric rush of my adrenaline from my head to toes. My mind was playing different scenarios as my senses searched for the best possible escape option with each scenario. The streets were all clear. There wasn't anything within a reasonable distance that was big enough for me to run to and hide behind without being spotted by the person or people coming out of that door. I then started to calm myself down. Running would probably send a panic around the police station and lead to even worse outcomes. So I kept my cool as the door opened and a female officer walked out. I studied her body language as soon as she set her gaze on me to see if I had any sign of distress or shock. She walked down the staircase as I walked toward her. She looked into my face as I approached her. She said hello, and I asked if it was possible to see a detective at that time. I could see that she picked up the confusion and fear in my voice. Then she asked me to go inside the station and talk to someone at the front desk. I agreed by nodding. Then she quickly walked past me. I climbed onto the staircase very slowly as I thought of how I was going to break the story to them. As I thought about how I was going to say it, I found it sounded a little far-fetched. Then I figured even if I talked to someone past the front desk staff, he or she would probably interrogate me and ask if I had taken any heavy drugs and then refer me to a psychiatrist. I imagined they would even take me into the mental clinic by force and give me medications that would start altering my normal brain. For a second I welcomed this outcome, but as I climbed the stairs, my paranoia was blaring like an ambulance alarm. I figured coming to the police station would be the most if not only logical thing to do for anyone in my situation. So I figured the attackers had probably already anticipated me being here. I considered the possibility of the cyberattackers walking me into a building that they were planning to blow up the moment I stepped inside. After all, they had asked me to make a post about a plane that they probably took down or were planning to take down. I figured I was pretty much cornered. So I started backing up and then turned around and strode off into the street and headed back to my apartment. Once again, I peered through every dark alley and every shadow, my ears listening to every sound and my nose searching for any distinct smells in the air. At this point, my fear had escalated beyond my ability to contain it. I was coming to terms with the fact that I was going to die. They had me in checkmate position. I had no words to say to help with my situation. I got into my apartment, and I started contemplating how each minute could be my last because I hadn't complied with the cyberattackers' demand and they meant business. I contemplated the many different ways that they might kill me. Maybe they would blow up the building I was in. That thought got me up from my couch. I felt a sensation of my blood boiling and my skin falling off my flesh. And suddenly, I felt like running back outside, but then I thought about being taken out from a distance by a bullet to the head. I was stuck. I could not believe that I was about to meet the end of my life just like that. Then my mind started spinning. How could I have let this happen? Was it the money I owed? Did I sleep with someone's wife? I searched my memory for any possible thing that I did, but my conscience was clear of anything that warranted an attack of such magnitude. I then thought of how the day had begun with condemnation from a radio station. I thought of all the other condemning things that I could remember people saying to me, and my mind supplied an abundance of such memories to make this situation seem deserving. Then I thought of what the preacher on the radio had said about how I had rebelled against God.

These thoughts were sealed when the pastor told me that he had seen me going to hell. I concluded that they were all right. All of those people I could remember telling me I was nothing and deserved to suffer were all right because I had arrived at this particular destination, I felt like I had now arrived in hell and all this was just the beginning. My apartment suddenly started to feel malevolent. I was now beginning to feel like the main character in the horror movie called *1408*. I figured that maybe sleep was a better idea to unwind my mind and help these seemingly uncontrollable emotions and fears subside. But as soon as I closed my eyes, dark memories rose to the surface with increasing intensity. I was completely frozen as I lay, expecting death by fire from an explosion or men bashing through my door with automatic weapons and riddling my body with bullets. I picked up my laptop and looked at Facebook. I always had to be doing something, so as soon as I recognized one of the cyberattcker's streams, I started responding with posts to let him know that I was recognizing his Facebook footprints. And then I was frozen all night, trying to sleep but being awakened by every small sound, some of which were just in my imagination, I'm sure.

When morning came, I wasn't sure whether to welcome the new day or to avoid it. I was so tired and wanted to try to rest. At the same time, I wanted to get out of the apartment and run, but none was possible. The cyberattackers had continuously kept on passing streams upon streams of mockery into my newsfeed. I had already gotten used to their ever-present mark in my newsfeed, so I paid less attention this time. The trouble was with the damage done to my mind. I was surprised to have lasted the night and still didn't want to die, so I started making more apologetic Facebook posts to them. My posts just attracted more comments from my friends, so I logged out and sat on the couch tired to fall asleep. However, I also wanting to stay awake to keep track of all happenings and try to make sense of all this. It was really windy outside and cloudy, so I couldn't even see the sun. Then the weather changed to a windy rainstorm. I had stayed indoors too long, and I was starting to feel claustrophobic, so I figured going outside would do me some good. I figured the windy rain would be camouflage against any possible attacks or shots from a distance. As soon as I walked outside, I could feel the wind blow on my face. I walked around different streets, my clothes getting drenched like I had just stepped out of a pool. As a police car was driving passed me, my senses heightened as I looked through the windshield, studying the two officers' body language. As it drove away, I logged it in my memory and walked on, rain pouring down on me and the wind still blowing. As I turned onto another street, I saw the same police car that drove passed me moments ago, and the police officers gazed at me. I quickly looked another way as I continued walking. I reached the end of the street and looked in all directions. I didn't see anybody, and then I screamed and screamed. I could feel my throat getting sore. And then I started to walk back home. As soon as I got back into the apartment, my fear, paranoia, mistrust, and paralysis kicked back in. The anguish of the uncertainty was so severe that I started walking around the apartment, sitting down, and then walking again. After a few hours, I ended this loop of walking around by logging into my email account. One of my friends asked if I could meet him at the city new library. It occurred to me that I met him recently at a multicultural event that involvement religious talks, and I did verbalize some of my deepest thoughts about global issues. I wondered if my presence at this event could have been the reason for all this happening. There were many religious leaders at the event, so maybe the pastor who made the radio program was also present at the time. Moreover, my friend who was asking to meet me was a retired government employee, and in the midst of all that was happening, anyone who worked with any government was a suspect. I didn't care if that person's job was just to make coffee. So I decided to go meet my friend at the library and try to gather any information that could explain all this.

It was not raining or windy anymore. As soon as I got out of the apartment to take a fifteen-minute walk to the library, I saw my cousin who had come to see me the day before. He was outside in his car parked on the side of the road like he was waiting for somebody. It was quite the coincidence that my cousin just happened to be outside when I needed a ride. I walked to his car and tapped on the window. He was slightly shocked to see me there coming out of nowhere. Then he asked how I knew that he was outside. I told him I didn't but that I needed a ride if he could afford to give me one. He told me to get in the car, and I did. I then started thinking that this coincidence was some kind of setup, especially since my family members were accomplices to this attack. When we got to the library, I quickly got out of the car and walked in. It was my first time there since it had opened. So I took some time to marvel at the great architectural and interior design. The coloring and the décor brought out this aura that inspired the mind to read and write or use one's creativity and imagination. But I cut my sightseeing short because of the gnawing need to figure out my situation once and for all. I looked at one of the information display screens in the lobby, and I found a message made out to me. At first, I didn't believe it, so I looked around and then looked back on the screen. The text change and told me that the message was really for me. Again, I looked away, not trusting my senses, and as I looked back, there was it was—the cyberattackers' signature. Then I knew that they were actually watching me. This moment completely made me forget my earlier thoughts of meeting my friend here. The message changed and asked me to go to a different floor, so I walked up the stairs to that floor just to catch the next text on a display. This one asked me to go to a certain section of that floor. So I complied and went to that section. Again, I found a display screen that said they were just joking, and then they asked that I go to another floor. This went on as they made me move around the entire library. I went along with this in hopes of finding the people who had attacked me. After some time it was clear to me that they had once again hacked into the surveillance and display system of the library. I saw a news crew doing a report as I walked past them. After this, I quickly walked out of the library and onto the street. On my way I wondered if my friend had asked to come to the library to draw me in the open so that they could take me out. Then the fear of being shot or jumped from a corner took over my mind again. I got into my apartment with tons on my mind. I was convinced beyond a reasonable doubt that they had hacked into my workplace surveillance systems as well. I logged into my email account just to find messages from my friend who had asked that we meet at the library. The first one was him letting me know that he had arrived at the library. The second one told me which floor to find him on, and in the third one, he asked if I was coming or not since he had waited for a few minutes. Other messages asked me where I was again. I then dismissed my earlier suspicions of him. I had no cell phone, so I was only communicating efficiently with friends through emails and Facebook. I had my friend's number and was planning on calling him from a pay phone at the library to find each other, but I got distracted by the cyberattackers' messages on the display screens.

It was scary that I was dealing with people with the capability of hacking into two of the most popular buildings in town like it was child's play. The government was still my number-one suspect. At about 3:00 p.m., the door to my apartment opened. I could feel and hear my heart pause as I pondered who might be coming through the door. Thousands of possible scenarios played in my mind, but then my cousin emerged from the stairwell again. He walked into the living room. I was now beginning to question if it was really coincidence when I found him in the car parked across my street, and then I remember him telling me he knew about my situation. My earlier suspicions of my family being involved in all this were heightened. I also considered him the cyberattackers' operative sent to finish the job of killing me. My cousin then sat down on the couch in the same spot as he had the day before.

This time I was studying his body movements and speech variations a little bit more intensely than I had with the other pastor. I was completely in fight–flight mode. He was also watching me, but he seemed more confused as if he was trying to figure out what was wrong with me. He then asked me how my library trip was. I replied with one word, simply saying that it was okay, while I pondered the many reasons why he would be asking me. He then started talking about life and experiences. Under normal circumstances, I obviously would have been bored by that conversation and asked that we play some music videos, but I listened anyway, hoping that he would get to the point soon and reveal some important information. I felt like I was in a distant realm and his presence there represented the human realm. Every piece of information he said was a representation of what the people actually thought of me. He talked on and on as I remained quiet and listened. Then I looked at the webcam on the computer and realized that it was still on. Somehow leaving it on gave me comfort, even though I knew the people watching were hostile. I looked at it as I thought more and more about the cyberattackers. Then I grabbed my laptop on the table and logged into my Facebook while I was listening to my cousin. I was also listening to his breathing patterns and the friction sounds between him and the couch. I would know about any slight sound changes before he could even make a move.

I had a theory that I needed to test. If the cyberattackers were watching us, they would let me know through the newsfeed. And in two minutes they signaled with posts in my newsfeed. They posted a message that said I should pay full attention when someone is talking to me. That was conclusive evidence for me, but this brought up a whole range of questions, considerations, assumptions, and scenarios. My cousin must have noticed a reduction in my attention as he interrupted my thoughts by getting up from the couch and walking around the table. He stood between me and the TV, blocking the webcam on top of it. I was watching him as he moved closer to me. He then stopped and stood above me about two feet away and continued talking. I sat there as alert as a spitting cobra with hood spread, ready to protect itself. My grip on my laptop tightened. I was ready to use it as weapon should he pull out a gun or knife. He went on talking and talking. I hoped he would get to the point soon because my patience was wearing thin. He then stopped talking and decided he was going to leave. I said okay and gladly walked him out the door, relieved about the way it had turned out. I could also finally get back to making further investigations.

I was still very much convinced that death was coming for me, so I went over some messages in my Facebook inboxes. It felt like I was looking at them for the last time.

Friends and family from my country were concerned and worried. I replied to a few messages from some really close family members and friends. My sister was the most worried, so I told her to disregard anything that she saw on Facebook. I assured her that I was okay. Then I replied to two of my best friends from home, telling them not to worry. I explained to them that I was being attack on the internet by some unknown people. One of my friends asked if I was at all involved in any crazy political matters. He reasoned that to be the only thing that would make me a target of a cyberattack of such intensity. I told him that I wasn't involved in any politics. I felt a little bit better after these interactions, but the unrest returned as I started to see more hacked streams from the cyberattackers. This time I wanted to text my close friends and family and tell them that I feared for my life because these people were planning to kill me, but I figured that would just make them worry. There wasn't much they could do to help with the situation. I figured that the attackers had already hacked my accounts since they knew I would be at the library. So if they were going to kill me, I had decided I was going to be man about it and not cause a panic. Besides, I figured that there had to be a way I could fight back. I started commenting on all the posts that I felt were from the cyberattackers. The comments did not make sense in terms of relevance to the actual posts. For example, a post that said something like "You're a loser" might have a comment that said something like "Amen" or "Hallelujah." I figured this was unpredictable enough to weaken the cyberattckers' grip. I also had a working theory that the Facebook mainframe categorized my footprint with the words, messages, comments, and friends lists that I made periodically. The best analogy I can give to how this works is what happens to people that are used to seeing you wearing suits all the time and then one day you suddenly dress casual. I figured that the Facebook mainframes would pick up any kind of discrepancies with the logged activity in the system, analyze it, store the data, and determine the best new footprint for those conditions. So by rapidly making irrelevant comments over an extended period of time all over the cyberattackers' posts, I hoped to change my Facebook footprint and see how that affected the methods of the cyberattackers. The one and only reason that I kept the comments positive was to avoid the risk of offending a real friend just in case of a mistake. So even with posts that talked about dying and going to hell, I still commented with nicer but irrelevant statements like "I love you too." I could see how all this was changing my Facebook home screen. I then logged out and started walking around the apartment. I looked out the window and saw that it was dark. I tried to anticipate the cyberattackers' next moves. I still could not shake the feeling that they would soon send someone to finish me off, so I figured taking precautions was a good idea. I turned on the lights in the apartment, all except the ones in the bedroom, where I stayed. I was slightly comforted by the lights being on. It might look like I wasn't alone inside. Moreover, as I stayed in the dark room, I watched the light underneath the door for any reductions, indicating a presence. The other advantage was that if someone came into my dark room, he or she would need time for his or her eyes to adjust and refocus in order to see me clearly. This little time would be enough to take defensive action. This was all I could do as I lay in my room in perpetual fear and panic.

Then the bell to my door rang, and my heart started racing like a super car in its last gear. The second ring got me up from my bed. I opened the door slowly and walked into the living room, thinking of who that might be and what to do. I looked out through the window, and I saw that the street was clear with no cars. Outside, it was quiet like an abandoned town. The doorbell rang again. Then I thought that maybe it was just one of my people coming to visit me considering my situation. The bell rang repeatedly, and then I started walking down the stairs. Different scenarios played in my mind—a bullet to the head, a knife to my chest—as I slowly opened the door. Standing in the doorway was a friend I had met a few years ago. We were quite close, and so my guard wasn't as high as the last time people had visited me. I felt I could trust him, and for the first time since the attack had begun, I felt a lot safer. He sat down on the couch in the same spot that my cousin had sat in earlier. I knew he was obviously worried and concerned just as everyone else was, and I felt like telling him every detail. I could hear his disappointment with me as he spoke. He asked why I was doing all this. I wasn't sure exactly what he meant by "all this." So I waited for him to continue. He asked if I was doing all this because I had been kicked out of a bar the night before the morning of my attack. And then I remembered that the last time I had seen him and some other friends from my country was the night I had been kicked out of a bar for some issue to do with the police coming to arrest me at the same place months before. I recalled that it was a very embarrassing moment as my friends watched me escorted out. And then it occurred to me that it was more than obvious that he had seen my Facebook rants and had wondered what was going on with me. I figured that was probably what he was talking about by "all this." But I could not believe he considered the bar incident reason enough to trigger my outbursts. As a matter of fact, I began feeling a little bit disappointed that someone I had been so close to for all these years would think that about me. I don't fuss or respond emotionally to small things like getting kicked out of a bar. My plate was already full with big things to worry about. But I said nothing because I knew that expressing my disappointment was what got me in this situation with friends and family in the first place. I wanted to tell him what caused me to act out that way, but before I could say anything, he said that I was acting as if I had no soul. I was now starting to feel as if I needed to build up wall of defense. I wondered why my friend would say something like that. I was now beginning to get angry, especially with myself for allowing people to tell me whatever they felt like saying. I looked at him as he continued talking. In the back of my mind, I was dissecting our friendship. Maybe I would pick up some information about him being an accomplice of the cyberattackers. My family was also involved, and he was well acquainted with some of them anyway. I decided he was an accomplice and that his words were just a malicious plot to compromise my strength further. The amount of disappointment I felt increased my anger, and I was tempted to attack him physically and interrogate him for details about the cyberattack. But with the lessons from how my outbursts led to such confrontations from friends and family, I restrained myself so that I didn't made things worse. He then got up from the couch to leave, but he asked why I had the lights on in the entire apartment. I couldn't give him an answer, so he asked that I turn them down. To save myself from arguments, I just nodded, and then he walked out the door and on to the street. I quickly turned off the lights as requested and went to my room. As I lay there, I failed to find any peace. What my friend had said had taken a toll on my mind. I turned all the lights on in my apartment again, including my bedroom this time. I walked around the apartment, pondering the words my friend had said about me having no soul. I was now beginning to accept the fact that maybe I really didn't have one, but if I didn't have a soul, then how was I alive? The feelings of this situation being deserving and memories of all the bad things I had done, even the things I had thought of doing in the past, present, and future filled my mind. Then the words of everyone who had told me that I would meet with a bad ending clamored in my mind. If I had no soul, maybe I was a ghost or a demon in the flesh. Those were my first considerations as I remembered the many life-and-death situations I had experienced throughout my life, though I had never even broken a bone like many normal people did. I then started remembering the many troubles I had gotten into as a kid. Some parents in the community even asked that I not hang out with their kids. Now I felt like a curse that had been born to this world. As if all this wasn't enough, I thought about how I could be a possible AI or robot. That would explain my physical ability to escape death. This information came from my knowledge of the many documentaries, movies, books, and TV shows about robots. More and more thoughts filled my mind until I started to convince myself that I was actually a robot. But I then I tried to dismiss this as I recalled my background. I was born from a man and woman, and I had siblings. But what if my creator had handed me to my parents already and instructed them to raise me exactly the way they did in order to make me believe that I was born from them and belonged to that family. But again, I dismissed this thought, given the genetic characteristics I had clearly inherited from my parents. Then I started to consider another possibility. What if everything I thought was part of my background was not real? What if it was a program meant to give me the impression of human identity with a background? What if I was a fresh robot created like a week ago, and before I had even opened my eyes, a story had played in my mind to serve as my background. And why all this cyberattack was happening in the first place? Maybe everyone in the world knew I was a robot. Perhaps that was why they didn't seem to care about what they said. That was why I was alone in this crisis. At this point, I was convinced beyond doubt that I was a robot. Then I started thinking of the studies suggesting that the most intelligent robot so far had an intelligence comparable to a bug. I was beginning to marvel at my creator's intelligence, imagination, and technology to create a robot of such sophistication like me, given the many qualities embedded in my programing—self-awareness; the ability to feel love, pain, fear; and the creativeness to imagine and make art. My newfound appreciation of my creation gave me a bit of respite from the torment I had experienced earlier, but it also began arousing my curiosity in a very dangerous way. There was gnawing thought about how I could prove that I was really a robot. I lifted my left hand and pressed it on my chest. The feel of my heartbeat through my hand gave me a conclusive end to the question. I was human, and I truly had a soul. Then another surge of doubt shot through my mind. Maybe what I felt was just a mechanical device designed to mimic the beating of a real heart. This left me filled with the uncertainty. I wandered the house in panic about my existence in this world. An idea then came to my mind. Humans had blood, so I could check to see if I had it too. With the nails of my left thumb and index finger, I squeezed a small part of the skin at the back of my right hand, and when the skin broke, I started to bleed. Given the pain I felt plus the blood I saw, I figured that had to be enough evidence to dismiss my doubt. I was once again convinced that I was human with a soul just like everyone else. However, there were still thoughts that lingered. Driven by impulse, I quickly decided that I would assuage my doubts. I reached for the sharpest knife in the kitchen. In that moment, I was ready to go all the way and prove to myself that my heart wasn't a mechanical device. But suddenly, I stopped when I remembered the story of Jesus when the devil was tempting Him to jump from the cliff of a mountain to prove that He was really the Son of God. This memory took over my mind. I snapped out of my daze and put the knife down. I had never appreciated or understood the power of belief until this time. My belief that I was human and the story of Jesus that I had spent so many days listening to at Sunday school brought me back to my senses. I then walked around the apartment, laughing. At first, I was laughing at myself. The devil's tricks had almost made me commit suicide.

I then walked into the living room and thought up another theory about everything that was happening. I reckoned that people following me when I was in another city wasn't about catching me in the midst of illegal activities. I figured they were watching me in order to study me, my behavior, routine, mannerisms, etc. They gathered up all sorts of information to use at precise moments. I concluded that they were using all of this data to come up with a strategy for an attack that would lead to one outcome, me committing suicide. I imagined that they had decided to set their attack in motion at a moment when I was the most mentally and emotionally venerable. I am no psychology expert, but I know the buildup of human emotions can lead to certain behaviors. And though I tried and failed to see it as coincidence, what better time to launch the attack than when I was grieving after that program on the radio about me and my work. They also had used my fear of being murdered to try to get me to claim responsibility for a terrorist plot. I figured it was an attempt to break my mind with fear and isolate me further. This would thereby encourage thoughts of suicide. I then began wondering why they would go through all this trouble to put this attack together. Then I remembered the many days that I drank recklessly, but I was only reckless enough to put myself in harm's way. Other than saying stupid things, I didn't drink and drive or physically assault anyone. I remembered a particular time when I was taken to the hospital for alcohol poisoning. When I was discharged, the nurse asked if I was trying to kill myself. Maybe that was the moment I was targeted. I figured that maybe after a few interventions, my family agreed to allow the organization to assist in my death as a last resort because they couldn't endure any more embarrassment given their Christian reputations. Everyone who knew me would allude to the drinking and drugs as early signs of my path to suicide without knowing anything about the cyberattack. Everyone at the funeral would then talk about how I was a troubled man with a troubled soul and how they had done everything humanly possible to help but that it wasn't enough to save me from myself. The cyberattackers would obviously offer to cover the funeral expenses, providing even greater incentive for my family to agree. The cyberattackers' payment for all this would simply be knowledge that their weapon could work. Then I remembered a Bible verse that said, "No weapon formed against you shall prosper." Next I remembered another that said, "My people perish because of lack of knowledge." With a chuckle, I imagined what would have happened if I didn't have the knowledge of Jesus's stories. I then walked to the webcam and started speaking to the cyberattackers through it, telling them that I knew their goal was to get me to kill myself. I said to them that if they wanted me dead, they should just come and do it themselves the old-fashioned way. But even if they end up killing me, I would still be the winner of this game. I then started laughing like a madman, pointing at the webcam, and said, "In your faces, you losers."

For the first time since the attack started, I was feeling confident with a certainty about things that I had never felt before. I had come to terms with dying. I sat down on the couch and started complaining about how I did nothing wrong except start a project to help helpless people. Then I talked about how the only wrong thing I did was get drunk, and if that was the reason I was being sentenced to death, then so be it. Nobody ever said life was fair anyway. I sat on the couch with a peach, waiting for someone to kill me. I even said to them that I would not fight whoever they sent. In my mind, I figured that there was just one me and too many of them, and I didn't want to get involve in a bloodbath. They say that before you die, your entire life flashes before your eyes. In my case, I thought about everything that I did and what I could have done differently. I had a few regrets here and there, but after a few hours, I had overcome my regrets. I had lived long enough, traveled, gone on adventures, loved, been loved, and conquered lots of fears and obstacles that I didn't think I could handle. I finally concluded that I had lived a rich life and that I would go into the next life with great happiness and joy. Even though orphaned and left in destitution, I was happy that my siblings were finishing school and living healthy lives with great prospects. I was ready to move on into the next life. Each minute seemed longer than a lifetime. Then my mind became quiet and calm.

This newfound tranquility was cut short by the sound of the doorbell to my apartment. I was jumpy all over again, but my emotions and fears were not as severe as before. I walked to the door, breathing heavily and ready to take on whatever came through, even if it was death. I opened the door slowly, and standing there was my pastor friend. But he was with a different pastor this time. I still was on high alert and paranoid, but I let them in, hoping that their visit wouldn't lead to more mental and emotional anxiety. They sat down on the couch across from me. I could see from their faces that they were analyzing me in an effort to figure out the best way to start the conversation. I paid only enough attention to show that I was acknowledging their presence. They asked me a few questions like how I was doing, if I had eaten, and if I needed anything. I answered their questions with a single word or a nod. My pastor friend then asked that we pray. They bowed their heads as I did, but I didn't close my eyes because I wanted to watch their movements. The prayer was short, and then my pastor friend asked that I say Jesus's name seven times. I first thought about the stories involving 666, the mark of the beast, that I had grown up with. Moreover, my pastor friend had always talked about how the world will be subject to the devil.

As I thought of the many reasons she would ask me to say that, it seemed increasingly absurd, given that I was faced with a real crisis involving this cyberattack. But I was still convinced that my pastor friend along with my family and the pastor who had made the radio program were working with the cyberattackers. Then my perspective on their motive changed, and I wondered if this was a religious game. I then remembered the pastor's words on the radio. He had said that I had rebelled against God.

I wondered if this had anything to do with my family's Christian heritage. The pastor on radio also knew that I had helped start a church in town and that I later stopped going to that church. Deep down in my heart, I knew I wasn't perfect, but I also knew that I was right with God. I was now beginning to grow suspicious. I felt that the rebellion the radio pastor spoke of was probably one against them or some political power. I had a sudden conviction that they were actually comparing themselves to the Lord or playing God. Then I thought about how the pastor had said that my writing would attract a large following but was not right in the eyes of God. I figured that was just a statement he made because of competition and territory. We live in a world of competing ideas, and maybe my ideas were a threat to his following. But weather this was all a religious game or a need to control me for some unknown reason, the odds were stacked too high against me. They were too many and too powerful, and refusing to say Jesus seven times might just make things worse. So I said it, and I saw a satisfying look on my friend's face. She then told me that if I had any weird thoughts or saw any strange things, I should just say Jesus seven times. I agreed, and then they took off.

Afterward, I wasn't as freaked out that someone was coming to kill me. I even imagined that there were people watching this and placing bets like it was a horse race. But I thought more of my losses in terms of damage to my reputation as a stable, sane man. There was also a possibility that some of the Facebook followers had caught wind of this incident and had completely lost confidence in what I wrote. I figured no one would want to read stuff from me, so I would have to give up writing altogether. Then I calculated that restoration would take the validation from systematic powers, such as religious leaders, psychiatrists, law enforcement, etc. The thought of the amount of bending I would have to do for these powers and the time it would take to get back what I had built was already tiring me. My worst nightmares were nothing compared to the experiences that this attack had brought.

As thoughts spun wildly in my mind, I figured it was best to lie down and see if I could get some sleep. I turned off all the lights in my apartment and went straight to bed. Just then the doorbell to my apartment rang, and I immediately wondered who it might be. But I didn't have the energy to deal with another visit, so I just sat where I was, thinking. The doorbell rang a second time breaking my train of thought. I had made up my mind that I wasn't going to open the door with so much on my mind. I figured that if it was one the cyberattackers' operatives coming to finish me off, then he or she would just have to do it the hard way, and that if it was one of my friends or relatives just coming to give me a piece of their mind, then they would eventually give up ringing the bell and go away. The doorbell kept ringing as I just lay there in my bed with my eyes wide open. Then the doorbell stopped ringing, and the silence that followed afterward was haunting. Maybe somebody had broken in. Then I got up from my bed and walked into the living room without turning on any lights. My heart was beating faster, and my eyes peered through the darkness, looking for any human figures, my ears listening for any sounds resembling footsteps. I heard and saw nothing except for my heavy breathing, and then I turned on the living room light and walked to the window. I peeped through it and didn't see anyone out on the street, and as I walked toward the kitchen area, the fire alarm went off, startling me. At this point I remembered the words my pastor friend said about saying Jesus seven times. But as I spoke, I thought about why my pastor friend would ask me to do this, Then I remembered that one of my cousins had emailed me and said I was having a Saul moment after I made the Facebook posts ranting against Christians and religious people. At the time that I saw the email, I thought my cousin was referring to the first king of the Israelites called Saul in the Old Testament, but it was becoming clear to me that he meant Saul the killer of Christians in the New Testament. Together with all this information, I also remembered that my cousin told me that Christianity was now dead on the day I made those rants. All this information was now starting to add up to one thing. I could not see it before because I was too caught up with the cyberattack. It was clear to me now that all this was nothing more than a natural Christian impulse after I had spoken ill of Christians.

I immediately became defensive. I wasn't just ranting about Christians. I spoke out against people of other religions as well as everyone in society. My cyberattackers had gone through a great deal of trouble to influence a Christian radio program by a pastor I listened to and obviously trusted. Then they attacked me on my Facebook moments after the radio program, knowing very well that all this was offensive enough and that I would connect the radio program with the cyberattack and speak against Christians and possible many other people, which is exactly what I did. The amount of precision required for this attack indicated that the cyberattackers were a specialized team that included people who knew about social behavior and psychology. I imagined that they knew that the magnitude of my reaction would ignite an equal amount of offensive action from my environment. All they needed was gather up some intimate information about me. They could be anywhere in the world and launch an attack through cyberspace and do massive amounts of damage that could even lead to deaths.

I began giving my friends a bigger benefit of the doubt now. I then logged back into Facebook and started making posts with sarcasm that only the cyberattackers could understand. Basically, I was implying that they were trying to use people to attack me without the same people knowing why, just like in the *Matrix* movies. All these people were saying these hurtful things without any knowledge of the battle I was fighting. I kept on making more subliminal posts to the cyberattackers until my friends started commenting on those posts, thinking that I was going crazy and making fun of that too. But I didn't feel angry or hurt this time because I knew that they didn't know what I was dealing with. It was clear to me that this was now a game of impressions. I figured I needed to do some damage control and avoid further confrontations from all the enraged people. So I posted that I was giving up my rebellion against God and that I was going to give my life to Jesus. I posted more about how I was going to follow God's teachings by going to church and listening to the preachers. I kept on posting more about my allegiance to God and my belief that He would protect me from anything. I went on and on until I could say no more. Then comments of encouragement started coming in, even from people I never expected to comment on my posts. They were congratulating me and encouraging me in the faith. At this time I realized those posts were enough to calm things a bit. I looked at the time and realized it was almost 5:00 a.m. I realized that I had been awake for the forty-eight hours. I was growing suspicious that this attack felt too close and personal. I then remembered that the construction crew had been doing renovations in my apartment. I wondered if they had taken something important or planted something incriminating in my apartment. So I started checking to make sure I had all of my important documents—my passport, immigration papers, and provincial IDs. Everything was there, and then I got onto my living room computer and checked for any suspicious files or documents, but I found nothing of significance. Then I started checking out everything that was lying around like pieces of paper, books, etc. After an hour of searching, I found a greeting card from a hotel that I had worked at more than a year ago, so I opened it to see what was written inside. It was addressed to my cousin whom I had once lived with in the same apartment but who was away on vacation with his girlfriend for a month. It made sense to me that the greeting card was addressed to him because he was currently employed at the same hotel. There was a sentence that was handwritten and signed by four women who were department heads at the time commending him for the great job he was doing. But what didn't make sense was a small piece of paper in the card that had typed text. It read exactly like what a friend had posted on Facebook about a week before. On the side of the card, there was a different handwritten word in a different color ink. There was also a small drawing of a smiling face that said, "Big improvement." I wondered if I was experienced déjà vu. I also wondered that how this would have been the weirdest coincidence. I didn't see any harm in considering this discovery. I had worked at the hotel for some years, and that was where I had met and had enjoyed lots of conversations with people of different cultures, professions, races, and religions. Maybe one of the guests I had met during the time I had worked there had started this operation, which eventually led to this cyberattack. I then wondered if one of the department heads that signed on the greeting card had anything to do with all this or if that card had really come from them. I acknowledged that all these were just speculations, but I was beginning to grow confident in my assessment of the cyberattackers. I wondered why they would want to make such a move. Was this all to let me know that they had been closer to me than I had originally thought? Or did they do this to drive me crazy with uncertainty? I pondered these questions with great intensity, but I wasn't sure of what explanation. I had found the greeting card in a remote corner of my apartment on top of my speakers. This area was away from the couches where everyone who had visited had sat. So it became clear to me that the greeting card was put there no earlier than a week before the attack began. I then started counting the people who might have had access to my apartment a week before. My cousin had a key, and the construction crew that was doing renovations had been inside too. These became the only possible suspects for people who could have put that greeting card there. I also weighed the possibility of an unknown individual I had never seen before breaking into the apartment and leaving the greeting card there. At this point, I realized it wasn't doing me any good to entertain thoughts of who the suspect might be because I would be looking into an ocean of possibilities. I figured that even asking would seem exactly like my rants and trigger more confrontations and cause more damage to my situation.

Then I was left stranded, not knowing what to do. I acknowledged how well all this was put together, which brought me back to my suspicions of the government working with my family. I then looked up my friend's post that I had found on the piece of paper in the greeting card just to be sure. I confirmed the comment word for word, and even my statements matched exactly. Then I decided that I would go to my former workplace at the hotel and speak to one if not all of my former department heads that had signed the card and try to pick up any information from them. I imagined that the only harm that would come from this action was them thinking I was asking some weird questions. Besides, given my losses, that was a small price I was willing to pay. It was now past sunrise, and I had already gotten over the fear of dying. I cleaned myself up a little, and at about 8:45 a.m., I was out the door and walked toward downtown with the greeting card in my hand. I still felt a shiver through my spine with each step I took because some of my Facebook friends were former coworkers that still worked at the hotel. I was convinced that they had obviously talked about the incident with other people at the hotel, so I felt quite embarrassed and timid. But my friends didn't fully understand the true reality of things, and that kept me going. There was something different about with the way I felt, and I could trace this feeling back to the moment I had put the knife down when I started believing that I was a real human. Overcoming of my fear of death had increased this feeling greatly. Everything was euphoric. It was like I could taste the air from my nose and mouth, and the light of the day seemed much denser with electrifying energy. As I walked, I felt like I was the main character of a really cool movie with a banging soundtrack. There was this feeling of freedom and hope that I can't describe with words. It was like I was walking on air and my feet were not touching the ground. I felt so good and so full of life. With these ecstatic feelings, I started considering that maybe I was in an alternate reality. I started to question if everyone around me was really as human as I was, I wondered if they were robots. I imagined that maybe we lived in a perpetual loop where at the touch of a button, everyone's minds would reset so that they did exactly as they had yesterday and the day before. I wondered what would happen the moment I arrive at the hotel. If this was a jump in reality, then maybe my old workmates wouldn't recognize me and think that we are meeting for the first time, even though I knew so much about them. What if they had been programed to recognize me by a different race or age? I was amused by all these possibilities, so when I arrived at the hotel after a fifteen-minute walk, I was a little more excited than normal to know once and for all if this was a time jump. At the front desk, my former coworker greeted me by name with the same sense of familiarity that she had showed me every day when we worked together. Another former coworker came from behind and greeted me by my name as well. At this moment, the time-jumping robot considerations I had made came crushing down. I was still in the same world, but the ecstatic feeling was still there. This even became a more uplifting moment because I now regarded every person as my equal in terms of humanity. My former coworker snapped me out of revere with a question about what I was doing there. I explained to my former coworker that I was just stopping by for a short visit. She welcomed that answer with excitement and told me that lots of my other former coworkers were in the back office, and then she led me there to see them.

I got to the back office and analyzed the area, noticing a few changes since the last time I had been there. Then I saw two of the department heads who had signed the greeting card together with another department head going into an office. They said hi as they walked past me, but I could see that they were busy. So I saw more of my former coworkers all greeting me with a warmth and excitement beyond my expectations. This brought a comfort I didn't expect. I stood there taking in the moment. I even forgot what I was there for. Then my former department manager greeted with a friendly smile. I had worked in so many departments, so I had lots of former managers. He then asked if he could do anything for me. I told him that I wanted to see either one of the four department heads who had signed the card that I had in my pocket. He then gestured that two of them were actually having a meeting with another person. Then he said that he could see me instead. I said yes. I was glad that he had asked because I didn't want to stand idle in the open office while everyone was working. We got to his office, and he offered me a seat. I sat down while looking around his office. It was a bit more packed than I remembered, so I made a comment. He said the clutter was because of the Christmas season, which made sense to me. Then he ask how he could help me. With as much strength and courage I could muster, I said to him that I had been going through something and that I just had a question about something I had found. I removed the greeting card from my pocket without the little paper printout and gave it to him. He looked at it as I analyzed his facial expression, hoping he would tell me something. But his reaction and words were casual, signifying that he didn't know anything about it. At this point, it was clear to me that speaking more about this wouldn't yield any significant results, so I responded by saying it was okay and that I needed to go. He was now puzzled and asked if I was sure, and I said yes. We got up and walked out of the office and into the lobby, where I asked my former coworker if I could wait there for one of the managers who had signed the greeting card. I specifically asked for one of my former managers in particular because I had a stronger friendship with her and felt comfortable talking with her about the details of my situation. Then my former coworker asked if I needed some coffee. Then it dawned on me that I had been awake and had not eaten anything for more than forty-eight hours, so I figured coffee was a good idea. I needed to be as coherent as possible. So I said yes, and she pointed to a coffee station near the front desk. It was in the same spot as it had been during the days I had worked there. As I was making coffee, my former department manager came to the front desk and started talking to one of the staff members about a fire drill starting in five minutes. I was close enough within listening distance, so I walked up to him and asked if they were having a fire drill. He said yes and pointed to an A4 paper-size frame on the at the edge of the front desk that said in bold letters that a fire drill would be conducted at 9:15 a.m. on December 1, 2016. And I remembered participating in a lot of fire drills when I worked at the hotel. We kept signs like that all over the hotel public areas to notify the guests to remain calm once the alarms went off. I walked to the couch and sat down with the coffee in my hands. Before I could even sip from my coffee, my thoughts and feelings made me shaky. The word *fire* brought back the same feelings I felt every time I thought the cyberattackers were going to blow up my apartment. The word *alarm* amplified these feelings even further as my paranoia grew. I then remembered the time the cyberattackers asked me to make a post about a plane going down and also use some Arabic words. The only real reason I was at the hotel was because of a greeting card that had allegedly come from the cyberattackers. It was now clear that explaining my presence at the hotel would sound very dumb and probably suspicious. My former peace was now devolving into an eruption as more thoughts popped up. The suspicions that I was being framed came back with intensity. I wondered if the cyberattackers purposefully planted that greeting card to lead me to the hotel. I imagined top management working with the cyberattackers from the very beginning. I imagined that the fire drill sign on the desk was a trick to make me believe that it was really going to happen. What if the operation to frame me was already in play? Operatives in the hotel could create a real explosion in the building, and then as the alarm sounded, some people would come rushing into the lobby and tackle me while I least expected it. Authorities would arrest me as the one who had caused the fire. Then I would go through a vigorous interrogation, and no one would believe my reason for being there. Law enforcement would then search my apartment, and the cyberattackers would have already planted more incriminating material there. And then the public outcry and media frenzy would play out. My friends and family would have no choice but to say that my earlier outbursts on Facebook were early signs of me committing this atrocity. They would all talk about how they came to visit to talk some sense into me but saw how caught up I was in my own dark world. After making these considerations, I suddenly began questioning the motives for all this. I was still convinced that it was governments working together. One of their possible motives might have been that they needed a villain to maintain their power and control over people. Maybe they had already evacuated the part of the building they planned to set fire to. They would say they had read the warning signs way back and started surveillance on me to learn my motives and thwart any move to hurt people. Individuals would receive medals. Politicians would be guaranteed reelections, and my family would possibly get a big check. I concluded that I would be locked up for the rest of my life and the people I knew would never speak of me again because of their anger and shame. This place, which I had found sanctuary in, was now becoming hostile. The only comfort came from the fact that I knew the truth of my innocence and that God was watching over me. Then I told myself that even innocent, pure-hearted people were targeted and hurt by the injustices of the unrighteous. I thought of how Jesus was killed, even though all He did was preach good news to the poor and perform miracles. It was then clear to me that truth and innocence weren't enough to shield me from the dangers I thought I was in. I needed to be smart.

At this time, I was convinced that I needed to get out of the hotel and not be in the building when that alarm goes off. As I got up from the couch, my former coworker told me that the former manager that I needed to speak to was on her way to her office. To me, this was confirmation of my suspicions that I was being framed in the hotel, so I declined and said that I didn't need to see her anymore. One of the department managers that knew me just happened to be walking by as I said this. She greeted me and asked me what I waiting for. Then she asked me if everything was okay. I said yes, trying to sound and look as assured as possible. She said okay. However, I could see the disbelief on her face as she looked into mine, and under normal circumstances, I would have stuck around to give her more assurance. But I just said I had to go and then started walking away. As soon as I got out of the hotel's front entrance and the glass sliding doors closed behind me, I heard the fire alarm go off. I didn't even look back. I strode off onto the street sidewalk. As I walked home, different thoughts occupied my mind. But I was comforted that regardless of the outcome of things, the truth always prevailed. At this time, I had a dying need to tell my close family and friends that regardless of what they heard about me, they should make their own judgments based on how I have been around them. But somehow, I knew such statements would be in vain. I would just make people more apprehensive, so I started focusing on being ready to face whatever would come. It might hurt or get me killed, but I wasn't afraid.

When I got home, the first thing I did was log into my Facebook, and given the experiences of the past two days, it wasn't hard for me to pick up on the cyberattackers' stream.

They were mocking me for going to the hotel. I wasn't surprised that they knew my whereabouts. How they knew of my hotel trip was now irrelevant because I knew they probably had operatives there or they had hacked in to the surveillance system. But I started thinking of the extent of their influence. The doorbell to my apartment rang. I didn't wonder much about who was at the door. I wasn't worried anymore about getting killed or being framed. Standing in the doorway were two police officers. I was surprised but not shocked to see them there. I had a feeling it had something to do with me going to the hotel earlier. I studied their body languages to determine the full extent of the visit. There was nothing about their behaviors that raised any flags. My words were the only threat in this situation. They greeted me and asked if they could come inside my apartment. It was weird that it was a request and not a command. I figured there was no harm in letting them inside my apartment, so I led the way until we came to the kitchen dining room area. I sat down on one of the dining chairs as the two police officers remained standing close to the staircase. The two officers looked around the apartment. The one thing that stood out in the room was the stack of empty beer and liquor bottles on a table in the kitchen dining area. One of the policemen had been the arresting officer in one of my public intoxication charges, so finding the bottles was probably no surprise to them. Then one of the officer's asked what I had gone to do at the hotel. I said to him that I stopped by to see my former colleagues. He looked at me, probably waiting to hear more, but I said nothing. An awkward silence followed, so the officers had to explain why they had come to my apartment. Turned out the former manager that I had spoken to in his office had called the police station out of concern for my well-being. The officer said that my former manager had said to them that I wasn't quite myself when I showed up at the hotel. I feigned a surprised look and said I was okay as they could see for themselves. He nodded in approval and asked what I was planning on doing the rest of the day. Then I told them I was planning on cleaning my apartment the whole day. The officer then said goodbye and left with his colleague.

After they left, I had much to think about. First, I was relieved that my suspicion about the fire drill was all in my head, there was a sudden feeling of comfort that followed because my former manager cared enough to call the police to check up on me. My trust in humanity was restored. I figured I needed to draw a line between the reality of my senses and mere speculation in my mind. The things I regarded to be true to both my mind and senses were the radio program that I had heard and the cyberattack that I had seen during the past forty-eight hours. As I broke information down between what I could prove with both my mind and senses and what was mere speculation, I felt like a detective working on a case. I figured that I would have to speak to the preacher in the radio program face-to-face and ask him about the inspiration for him to make such a program and try to pick up details from his story and behavior to solve my case. But I now understood how hard this was to accomplish given my lack of resources and broken reputation. Even if I managed to get a sit-down talk with him, he might deny that I was the subject of his program, given that he was careful enough not use my name. He could argue that he was talking about text that was just similar to mine. So whether he was working with the cyberattackers or not, I concluded that I wouldn't be able to get any helpful information from him. Plus that course of action also posed the risk of a counterattack from him. I was beginning to appreciate the cyberattackers' methods, and they might have been good enough to even make the radio preacher think it was his idea by subliminally flooding his computer and phone screens with my writing and waiting for him to pick it up and make a radio program. I then wondered if they did the same thing to make some of my friends say exactly what they said. I was beginning to understand the scale of planning that had gone into all this to make sure that they remained hidden. I figured that the most effective way to get to them would be through cyberspace. I figured they must have left tracks that could lead me to the source, but to do that, I would need an army of computers with the computing power to pick up those tracks in cyberspace. I knew my story was beginning to sound like alien conspiracies and flying saucers or mummies and vampires. I was becoming increasingly frustrated. So much damage had been done to me by people who were so far out of reach. I felt so small and bullied. I logged into my Facebook and found a message from the former coworker who had greeted me first at the front desk at the hotel. She said that she was there for me if I needed someone. I was comforted by this. I had some people who genuinely wanted to help. I wanted to tell her, but I didn't even know how to so. I just sat there speechless and helpless as I thought more and more about the damage they attackers had inflicted on me.

Then the doorbell rang. I felt like my house was becoming busier than a drive-through at a fast-food joint. Then the door opened, and I heard someone climbing up the stairs. My cousin walked into the living room and sat on the couch next to the one I sat on. I got up on my feet and walked toward the dining room area. He asked how I was doing, and I gave him a one word answer that I was okay. Then he asked what was going on with me. In that moment I had a major realization. I remembered him saying he knew exactly what was going on with me, and now he was asking this question. I asked what he meant, but his response was vague. It became clear to me that he had made an assumption about what I was going through. If he had known how I was going to interpret those words, he wouldn't have said them. With my cousin's words and our history of family tensions over the past few years and the pressure of the church and morals, I had started thinking that my family was somehow involved in this. It was now becoming clear to me that he wanted to comfort me when he first came to see me. Without hesitation, I begun telling him about the cyberattack, how it was done, and how it got me to react the way I did. I even gave him the Ernest Rutherford analogy of how I didn't know my friends would end up seeing my posts. And I also mention how the computer was taken over through the IP address and how the cyberattackers tried to get me to make a terrorist post on Facebook. I said all this with a plea in my voice, asking him to believe me. It took him awhile to let all this sink in. Then he asked with a great sense of confusion why I had responded. He explained that the internet was full of malware and fake posts that prompt people to react to them. After this statement I knew that he was looking at this as just a normal cyber pranks. I told him it wasn't one of those normal pranks. I explained to him the information they had about me was very personal. I told him they knew things I had never told anyone before. I even told him of the time someone was following me in another city. He then said that an attack of such strategy and intensity was usually reserved for individuals of influence and great stature. I agreed. That was why I was so freaked out. Then I told him that this was why I was acting the way I had been. It was not some spirits or ghosts or demons taking me over. I then told him that maybe the reason had to do with the Facebook page I was running. Or maybe I had hung out with someone on a terrorist watch list during my many nights out and was pegged as a possible accomplice because of that association. I told him all this, even though I knew that he found it too far-fetched, but I didn't care. I just needed to tell this to someone at that time. He then decided to leave, and I walked him out the door. Afterward, I sat down to do some more critical thinking. I concluded that my family was not at all involvement in any of this. I figured I still had some more damage control to do. Showing up for work would deem me stable and deescalate the impression people had that I was crazy. As I walked to work, I still felt a great deal of shame because of the things I had said in my rants. I also started feeling more embarrassed as I got closer and closer to work. I was met with a few stares from my workmates upon arrival. I didn't feel comfortable sitting in the employee room, so I walked straight to my supervisor's office. I sat down across from one of the supervisors I had seen the night the attack had started. The other supervisor from the night was also in the office. He turned some of his attention toward me, probably wondering what my situation was exactly. Then my supervisor started going over tasks he wanted me to do, but as I listened, an apprehension was growing in me. I was in the building I knew the cyberattackers had hacked. They were probably still be watching as I worked. So before my supervisor could finish, I cut in and said that I didn't think I was fit to work that day and that I needed to sort out some personal issues first to do a good job. He agreed with me and didn't ask for more details. It wasn't surprising to me either that he was going to give me time off, especially since my Facebook dilemma had spread to almost everyone who knew me. Besides, there was also the state of my behavior when I came in to see them. He then said that I could take as much time off as I needed, but I couldn't take longer than two weeks. That was much more than I was expecting to get, so I quickly said okay, thanked them, and left.

When I got home, I still could not shake the feeling of shame and embarrassment. The best thing I could do to alleviate the situation was nothing. Everything I thought of doing would really only make my predicament worse. I then called one of my close friends. He said he was hearing a lot of stuff about me from people all over, and he kept asking me about what was going on with me. I tried explaining some things, but I could hear my own incoherence as I jumped from topic to topic. After I hung up from that call, I thought about how I might have been cursed by a witch from stepping on a wrong place. Or maybe I was paying for a wrong I had done in another life. After a while, I could not handle the way my mind was haunting me. I felt like calling someone to talk to, but I was too embarrassed and ashamed to talk to any of my friends or family members. Besides, they all thought I needed special treatment, so I figured the conversations weren't even going to be real. It was dark outside, and I felt it was a good idea to go out for a walk so that I could have the space and time I needed in that moment. As soon as I stepped down the concrete stairs, I saw a girl across the street smoking a cigarette. I realized that a conversation with a total stranger might help me calm down. I looked at her to see if she would be open to conversation. I had never seen her before, and it was a bit weird that she was just standing there, smoking a cigarette. I wondered if she was waiting for someone or just waiting to finish her cigarette before she was on her way. And then I told myself that I wasn't going to overthink this. I would just go over and talk to her. Besides I really could not afford to put any more pressure on my mind. So I walked up to her and said hi, and she said hi back. Without delay, I mentioned that I had been in the house for too long, so I came outside to find a fellow human being to connect with. She smiled and tilted her head. She must have thought of it as a pickup line or a smooth joke. Somehow her smile compelled me to do the same, and then I realized that was the first genuine smile I had given in days. I hadn't even really smiled before the attack. She then threw the cigarette bud on the ground and gently crushed it with her foot. I asked what her name was. She told me and asked for mine. Immediately after I told her, I felt ashamed and embarrassed again. Maybe she knew my name. I knew how quickly gossip could spread in such a small city. Her face showed no signs that she knew about me though. I could not hide the amount of joy I felt because she didn't know me. I must have started smiling. I realized that I needed to come up with a logical explanation why I was smiling, but I could not stray from the truth. I said to her that I was just surprised that she didn't know me or that she hadn't heard of me before. She looked at me with a facial expression that suggested she thought maybe I was egotistical. I really did want to tell her the real reason I was happy that she didn't know about me. But that was too complicated to explain, and I didn't want to ruin this moment of respite. So I figured I would just play along to keep the conversation going. So I told her that I was a big shot and that people all over town knew me. Then she asked why I was known. I knew that this was escalating and that this situation would blow up in my face. So I said to her that I had made a huge scientific discovery and how there was chatter about it was all over town and that I was about to make international science headlines. As I said this, she started smiling, probably thinking that it was one of my pickup lines or jokes, but her smile faded as what I had said sunk. I had said the words with a surge of belief in my voice, probably because of my inability to control my emotions. I knew this conversation had turned to awkward territory and I needed to bring it back so that we could have a normal adult conversation. I didn't want her thinking that I was a child in a grown man's body or a lunatic. So I answered her question by asking her to guess how old I was. She went right ahead and said twenty-five. I was glad that she didn't say twelve because I would have taken that as an insult. I gave her a face that said, "You can do better than that," and pointed my index finger up. She said twenty-six, and I made a face that said, "You miss again," and then pointed my index finger up again. She said thirty, and then I pointed my thumb down until she counted down to twenty-seven. She was smiling again, and I felt good that I had dodged a bullet there. She then asked me to guess her age. When I first saw her, I guessed that she was probably in her early twenties, but I didn't say this out loud. I knew that if I was ever asked to guess a woman's age, I didn't want to guess higher than her actually age. It doesn't matter whether you're George Clooney or Will Smith. You'll find yourself on her bad side if you guess too much. So I said eighteen just to play safe. She looked at me, smiling with excitement, and she shook her head to tell me I was wrong. I could tell she was flattered. I smiled back, getting ready to guess again. Now I could have chosen to go lower, but I didn't want her to catch me playing it safe with guessing her age, which would probably just annoy her. So I ended up saying nineteen, and she still shook her head, laughing, her face glowing in that moonlight. I said twenty, and she laughed even more, shaking her head as I laughed along too. Then I told her that I gave up and that she should just tell me. I said I wasn't good at the guessing game and didn't want to embarrass myself further. She said she was twenty-three. Things were going smooth again now. So we talked some more about our life experiences and our backgrounds for the next ten to fifteen minutes. I told her that I was having a lot of fun with her, and I said that if she felt the same way, we could go into my apartment and spend more time together. I pointed at the townhouse. I told her that I didn't live too far to walk. I could see in her eyes that she wanted too, but then she looked me deep into my eyes and asked if I was going to do anything to hurt her. I understood her concern. After all, we had just met, and I was a total stranger. But I walked a bit closer to her and said I wasn't the type who hurt women purposefully. The worst I could do was probably bore her or say something that would make her think she was hanging out with someone who was stupid. She took a moment and looked me over. Then she said okay, and we walked to my building. We got into my apartment and stopped at the dining area. I could tell that she was scoping out my apartment, and then I realized I still had the many beer and liquor bottles out on the table. I looked at them and told her I had had a lot of friends and some family over lately. I quickly apologized. Had I known I was having a guest, I would have made the place look spotless. She must have sensed that I was a bit embarrassed and said it was okay. She said she didn't mind because she was happy just being there with me. I said okay, and we sat on the dining table chairs. Then I realized that I needed to offer her something to drink, so I walked over to the refrigerator and opened it. I had not gotten groceries in a while, and I had been eating out a lot, so I didn't have any snacks or drinks. I fidgeted around, thinking about how embarrassing it was that I had brought her in my apartment, which didn't have anything other than water. So I looked at her and apologized and explained how I would have prepared better had I known she was going to come over. She said she was okay and told me not to worry about it. My body language still showed that I was still beating myself up about it. Then she said that I was really handsome. I really appreciated the classiness she portrayed in trying to build up my broken confidence. So I sat on a dining chair next to her, and in less than a minute, all that existed was that moment. We talked and talked until we became increasingly slower and slower. Our voices got quieter and quieter but deeper and deeper until we fell into intense intimacy and passion. Afterward, she said she had go. I said that I was hoping she would stick around so that I could cook some food and we could eat before she left. She told me she would have loved that, but she had stayed longer than she should have and needed to go now. I said okay and then started to walk her out while we exchanged Facebook information. I explained to her that I hadn't gotten a new phone after the last one broke when I fell down the stairs some months before. She laughed, and I laughed along with her, remembering the many empty beer and liquor bottles she had seen. I then told her to just ring the bell whenever she was in the area and wanted to see me. She said good night, and I did the same. She walked away, and I came back into my apartment.

Suddenly, my most recent moment of respite and passion was now starting to devolve into one thought—*sin*. Earlier in the day, I had declared that I was a born-again Christian and that I would follow the teachings of the faith, and then hours later I was fornicating. The whole thing was hypocritical and blasphemous to God. My feelings of guilt started coming back to me. I remembered every word in the radio program and how the other pastor had said he saw me going to hell and how my friend had said that I had no soul. I started thinking that they were all right. I had sinned hours after declaring on Facebook that I would follow God. Then I thought about all the times I did or said something wrong, the many troubles I had gotten into, and the mistakes I made. At this time, I thought God's wrath and vengeance on man. I was now convinced that I was beyond redemption and that God would soon come down Himself and throw me into the lake of fire. The terror in me now was much stronger than it had been with the cyberattackers. God, whose size extended beyond the universe, was coming to strike me down with extreme fury. There was not a single place I could go. I felt rejected by society and God. Not even the grave was safe. I just sat in my apartment for hours as I felt tormented. What happened next is still beyond my understanding, and I will possibly never know exactly what happened. But in the tiniest corner of my mind, there was a thought that started as a little spark and grew. My previous fears and pains had been unnecessary, and so I asked myself, "If God was really going to punish me for fornicating, why hadn't He done so the first time I had sinned that way?" I had fornicated with lots of women, going all the way back to my boyhood, and I had been declaring that I would stop sinning and follow God's teachings all my life. So I wondered why He didn't condemn me any time before now. Once again, I remembered I had to keep what I thought in check. I recalled the many Bible verses that talked about God's forgiveness, grace, and salvation. I knew that the scriptures said that God loved the world so much that He had given His only Son to us and that humans killed Jesus, who later forgave them. I imagined the horrors I would inflict on someone who hurt one of my family members, but God instead chose to forgive humans for killing His Son. So why wouldn't the same God forgive me for the things that I did, which were nowhere close to killing His Son? Furthermore, I remembered that our salvation from hell comes by God's grace and not our own doing. That's when I realized how severely affected I was by this cyberattack and how I had been giving people too much power and credit. If a being who was bigger than the universe came to strike me down, I was certain that it would not be the God that I worshipped and that I would stand my ground without fear regardless of how small or powerless I seemed, knowing that the God I truly believed in would provide the protection I needed. With this newfound realization, all the feelings of shame and guilt that I was feeling crumbled as my assurance that I was a child of God increased. I was now starting to see certain facts that I had missed when this attack began. I was giving people too much power over my life, and I ended up almost losing my faith, life, and sanity. I acknowledged that I was alive not because I was smart, strong, or faithful but only because God was allowing it. I acknowledged that what was happening was nothing more like a kindergarten drama. The pastor who had made the radio program, the cyberattackers, the friends and family and every other person were just people with minds and hearts that could break like mine. Just because they say they speak for God doesn't mean that's true. They are also subject to corruption and deceit. Only God knows the ultimate truth, and as humans, we can only understand a small part of it.

I decided I was going to fight the cyberattackers however I could. I grabbed my laptop and logged into my Facebook with a confidence and courage that I didn't have before. They fired a stream all over my newsfeed, and I responded tactically. This time I was much better at reaching out to them and cutting through their streams at pivotal points. This was like a game. With each successful attempt, the screen kept changing until I arrived to an elaborate platform that I never thought existed on Facebook. This was similar to an admin Facebook page, only this one was more complex. The platform was more like an open office with multiple members to fill up spaces and contact each other via chat text. There were tools and accessories similar to that found on other computers. There was a tool area where you could pick things like a pencil, brush, and rubber similar to those found in graphic design programs like Photoshop and Adobe InDesign. Alongside it, there was another area with labels of different types of images. The labels included topics such as religion, movies, sex, among others, and if I clicked on any of the labels, the corresponding program opened up with more options. The program does this over and over again until it narrows the search down to a precise image suitable for them to make a quick post. It was the same process for videos too. This platform also had built in video editing accessories like aftereffects. A person can make a quick post with a video of a famous person saying some words to the user's exact specifications. The platform also had a music area with music editing software. Basically, it was a Facebook platform with built-in creative software like the ones creative professionals buy and keep in separate folders on their computers. A post that would take ten days to build would take less than ten minutes to make in this platform, and that's just for a beginner like me. It was now starting to make sense how they were able to respond to my actions with such elaborate streams. They must have gathered up enough information on me and waited to attack with a certain precision based on the information they had. All they must have done was just compound my reactions and movements with more streams so that I would believe that they were steps ahead of me. A direct message came up on my platform like a Facebook chat pop-up. They talked about how they were a commercial organization with lots of opportunities and how they thought I could be a valuable member of their team. I was flattered by how people with such computing power, information databases, and creativity to portray illusions like they did would think of me in that regard. I thought of the many benefits being a part of an organization like this would bring. I would have access to their computing power and state-of-the-art creative software to promote my own private projects, including the Facebook page I was running. But somehow I felt disrespected by this offer, especially since it came moments after they had invaded my privacy. I was tempted to only say yes so that I could eventually meet them. It was kind of a cheap shot showing me this platform with all these accessories and state-of-the-art software. Given the amount of intimate information they knew about me, I figured they must have known about my graphic design activities as well, and they must have shown me this platform to arouse my interests. So I wondered if they really thought I was stupid enough to fall for this illusion. They had been playing with me since the beginning, and I knew this was just one of their many games. Even if this was a real deal, they had asked me to pose as a terrorist on Facebook, not caring about the consequences and damage that might the action would bring. Their cavalier attitude to wreak havoc was too much for me to handle, so I declined by saying that the only thing I cared about after everything that had happened was going back to my home country. Then they started repeating the offer more and more, but I kept saying no.

It was now seventy-two hours without sleep. I thought of going to the police, but I figured that the sound of this would send up red flags, given that police had arrested me for alcohol offenses before. They would have no problem suspecting that I was on drugs and seeing things. I figured getting at least one believable piece of evidence would make my story valid to the authorities. The offers didn't stop coming. I think they must have thought that I needed time to process all this and realize that given my financial status and prospects, their offer was the best to get me on feet. Then an idea came to me. I could play along with this game. I figured that if they thought I was stupid to fall for this, then maybe I could lure them into doing something that would compromise their position. So I said yes, but I made them guarantee that they ensure I could get to my home country since location obviously didn't matter. I wondered if they had the capabilities of easily honoring my request and getting me a flight just like that. They would get that flight for me either by buying it with a credit card or using cash or hacking into the airline's flight database. Then I would report this to the authorities and airline and give my story, and together, they would launch an intense operation to track the source of payment for that flight. This request must have gotten under someone's skin because I got what seemed like an aggravated reply. They were the ones that had come to me, so I replied politely with the same answer but with fewer words. The offers kept coming but with a bit of added sarcasm. I stopped replying and sat down, waiting. Maybe their ego would get in the way, and they'd be tempted to prove their power and fall for the trap. I even logged out of Facebook to show them that my decision was final. When I checked my online accounts, I noticed that my paycheck had come in, so this changed my mood a little bit. I logged back into Facebook and found more and more of their offer, so I replied with the same counteroffer, saying I had all the time in the world. So for hours we kept going back and forth until 11:00 a.m. when the offers ended and I got removed from the platform. Things went silent after that. All their streams had disappeared. I pondered what this development meant. Were they going to do it, or did they decide to move on? After waiting for more than an hour with no sign of their activities in my newsfeed, I logged out of Facebook and walked around the house, wondering what I should do. I had zero fear in me. I started thinking about everything that had happened the past three days and how they had said they were a private organization. I acknowledged the possibilities of a private organization launching stakeouts and gathering information to use against me and executing a complex cyberattack to make me feel isolated. I began considering other applications for this style of attack. The intimate information that they showed in the first stream was not incriminating, but it was annoying enough to trigger anyone that valued privacy to act irrationally. I considered how venerable this would make someone if the person believed that his or her most innermost secrets were revealed to the public. Most people would be willing to do almost anything to save themselves from the consequences of revealing that information because they feared the damage to their reputations or relationships. I imagined further how a person of power and influence can be easily targeted. Maybe like a police officer with lots of dirty secrets. Maybe that cop would be the target of a stream and threatened with exposure unless he or she shot an innocent person in public. Some people would commit such atrocities to save themselves. Others would simply commit suicide, and the investigations would not show any signs of third-party interference either. I then concluded that this was a terrorist organization aimed at causing havoc by preying on the weak, the broken, the guilty, or the rejected, who would do their dirty biddings while they hid behind the shadows of our communities. I wondered if this was also the case with the pastor who had made the radio program.

I was really hoping they would fall into my trap because I was itching to get to the bottom of all this. I then stopped because I didn't want to compound more negative thoughts, so I figured going outside and mingling with people would be a good idea. So I took a quick shower and changed my clothes for the first time in three days. I then walked out of my apartment and headed toward downtown. Being outside, I was ecstatic. It was like every atom in my body was having a party. I walked around free from fear and panic like a bird in a clear sky. I decided I was going to be outside that day and spend time looking at scenery. It then dawned on me that going for an all-day drive would be therapeutic. I didn't have a car, so I figured that I could try calling some friends or family and see who was available to take me for a drive, but I quickly dismissed this idea. My friends and family were still worried and offended, and that negative energy would just impede the tranquility I would get from looking at nature. And then it occurred to me that my cousin who was away on vacation had left his car in the parking lot and that I had access to his car keys at the apartment, and I had enough money for gas to drive the whole day. So I went back to my apartment and grabbed the keys. I also took my passport with me because that was the most important document I had and I didn't want it lying around in the apartment after everything that had happened. I locked the door and went straight to the underground parking lot. I got into the car and put the key in the ignition and tried to start it, but the car wouldn't start. I tried again a few times, but the engine still wouldn't turn over. I figured it was a power problem and that the battery was dead. I considered trying to jumpstart it with some cables and another vehicle, but I didn't have the patience. Plus I wanted to get to my sightseeing right away, so I got out of the car and locked it. I just walked along one of the busiest streets downtown. Then I saw a bus that was going to the airport, and I remembered that the route it took had lots of scenery. I welcomed the idea of being on the highway in a bus and just looking out the window like I used to when I was a kid. I ran after the bus, but I was too late getting to its next stop. I watched it as it drove away. I remembered that the city bus to the airport ran hourly, but I didn't entertain any thoughts of waiting because I was dying to get out to nature. I decided to take a cab. The ride was quiet, and I appreciated the cab driver's sensitivity in keeping it that way as I looked out the window the entire way. After forty-five minutes, we got to the airport. I wanted to keep on going, but after looking at the fare, I decided it best to stop there and pay. I wandered around the airport, remembering the day when I first arrived in town and how much time had passed and the things that had changed. For more than an hour, I watched the buildings, the planes, and the people making their way in and out the buildings with their luggage, and then I remembered that the cyberattackers had hacked into the surveillance systems of three different buildings in the city. I then began wondering if they had done so again with the airport surveillance systems and if they were watching me right now. I walked into the building and thought about this possibility. I figured that if they were watching me at the airport, then maybe they would take that as a signal of faith and they will fulfill my request. I walked around the airport, analyzing the premises and the people as well as the airport staff. I walked to the departure area and approached every airline counter to check if there was a travel arrangement for me. The airline employees checked and found nothing. I thought of trying another angle and asked them to check within the next event days. They checked and still found nothing. I didn't have a cell phone or computer, so I asked if there were any public computers anywhere in the airport. Then they told me that some hotels within airport premises had some computers that I could ask to use. I got to one of the hotels and went to sit at the bar as I thought and processed information.

Afterward, I went to use one of the computers, and as I logged into my Facebook account, I observed nothing in my newsfeed pointing to the cyberattackers. I logged out and came back to the bar. I was now starting to think that my recruiters had probably moved on to other candidates like me. Given their power and resources, I figured they had lots of options and didn't want to waste any time with me. I was both relieved and disappointed. All that was left of their existence was the damage they had done to me, and they were the only human witnesses that had seen everything. I had nothing, and my hopes of getting a piece of evidence dissipated. A bartender walked up to me across the counter and asked if I needed anything to drink or eat. Tt then dawned on me that I had not eaten for more than seventy-two hours, but what I really needed in this moment was a drink. She handed me a food menu quickly and went away to give me some time to decide. I stared blankly on the menu, disappointed that I'd never prove my story to anybody. She came back and snapped me out of my daze. Then she asked if I had made up my mind. I told her that my I didn't look at it much and asked her what she would recommend. She then told me that their kitchen was just opening for the day and that it would take a bit of time to get the food ready, but she offered to make me a quick meal with some of the frozen foods. I said okay, and she asked what I wanted to drink. I asked for some red wine, and she served me a glass right away. Afterward, she brought me a bowl of spaghetti, I sat there eating and drinking, taking my time as thoughts went through my mind. For hours I sat there as the bartender stopped by for a quick chat while she filled my glass whenever it was empty. I had worked in the customer service industry before, and there was no way that I could beat her style of service. At about 9:00 p.m., I settled my bill and ran off to catch the bus home.

As soon as I got home, I went straight to bed. The wine had given me a bit of a buzz, so I was feeling relaxed. Then the door to my apartment opened, and I heard someone coming up the stairs. I didn't bother with thoughts of who it might be or what they wanted. The comfort my bed and the aura in my room was all that mattered in that moment. Then the door to my room opened, and my cousin shouted my name. I lifted my head slightly to look at him as he turned on the light. But then I rested it on the pillow again. He asked how I was doing with a look of relief on his face. I said I was okay, and then he asked what I did all day. I replied that I was out and figured that he must have been coming by during the time that I was out. He just stood there as if he was trying to figure me out. Then he said I was giving them a full time job and had not slept from the pressure of my wellbeing coming from friends and family all over. I said nothing back. I remained lying down with my head on my pillow and my eyes open, blankly looking at the wall. He then said he had to go, and I said okay. It was now clear to me that I would have to leave whatever was left of the bubble before he opened my bedroom door to go in order to make sure the front one was locked. So I stood up and walked him out. With the tranquil bubble completely gone, the feelings of being beaten came back. I started feeling embarrassed. I picked up my laptop to try to keep busy. I tried to read or watch something, but my concertation kept turning toward social media until I found myself logging into Facebook. There was still no sign of the cyberattacker's posts or streams on my newsfeed. It now dawned on me that the cyberattackers had really moved on. Their game with me was over, and they were probably starting an attack with another unlucky individual like me. I felt like a lab rat that had been used for vigorous experimentation and then tossed back. I suddenly didn't feel like I wanted to participate in any social media activity anymore. The sight of it made me relive the events of the last three days. So I did what I felt was necessary to begin my healing process. I deactivated my Facebook account and spent the rest of the night trying to save my emails and other internet passwords. I had been up for ninety-six hours now. At about 9:00 a.m., there was a knock on my door, and the doorbell rang. I figured it was probably one of my friends or family members checking up on me. I opened the door, and standing in the doorway were two police officers. This time it was a man and a woman. I could not hide my shock when I saw them. In the back of my mind, I kept thinking that their visit had something to do with me being at the airport. They asked if they could come in. I quickly let them in, and they scoped my apartment. They stood in the same spot that the other two officers had a couple days before. The beer and liquor bottles were still there, and in the back of my mind, I started beating myself up for not removing them earlier. I knew my profile in their system showed alcohol offenses, and the presence of the bottles probably sent up some red flags. Then they told me that the reason they had come to see me. One of my family members had called and asked them to come check on me. I asked who, and they told me the name. The police officers then told me that my family member had gotten worried when they couldn't find me on Facebook and assumed that something had happened. I appreciated the warm concern of this gesture. I gave a loud chuckle and said wryly to the police officers, "All this was because someone could not find me on Facebook?" They said yes. The female officer then said it was probably because they cared so much about me and Facebook was their only way of contacting me. But I became increasingly frustrated and angry that things had escalated this far. Then the police officers asked me why I had deactivated my Facebook account, and a surge of suspicion returned. Maybe the cyberattackers were trying to use people around me to get me back on Facebook so that they could taunt me further. But I quickly dismissed this suspicion. My situation had caused things to progress this far. I told them that I had deactivated it because I didn't need it anymore. Then the female officer asked how my friends and family would reach me. That was exactly the reason I had to deactivate my Facebook account. Everyone was worrying about me and demanding answers that I didn't know how to give. Then the male police officer asked if I had thoughts of suicide. I was now filled with anger, frustration, and amusement at the same time. I wanted to laugh out loud, but I calmed myself down and said no. He then asked why, and then I told him assuredly that I wasn't the kind of person to think about suicide. I believed in fighting my battles. He nodded, and then the female officer told me that there were many resources and public facilities at my disposal to help with whatever I was going through. She then handed me a card and asked me to call the number if I felt the need to talk to someone. I said okay and thanked her. She then suggested that I reactivate my Facebook account to keep my friends and family from worrying and give them peace of mind. I laughed as she said this and said that I wasn't going to do that. As they could see, I was okay. They looked at me with confidence in my words and then left. After that, I realized that I had bigger problems to solve than worrying about the cyberattackers. Groups of people were convinced I had gone insane and needed professional help. Others believed I was possessed by a demon that needed to be exorcised, while others thought I was doing all this as a desperate attempt for attention. There were lots of different interpretations and stories surrounding my situation, which all started on November 29, 2016, but I wrote this to explain the full details of how events unfolded to the best of my recollection.

About the Author

Manson Mutumba's father worked in a cinema, so he grew up watching how movies were picked in relation to the moods of the community. At an early age, this sparked an interest in storytelling and scriptwriting as well as the fundamental aspects of the audience. He is currently a university arts student and a bit of a traveler.